LEARN TO READ

JONATHAN JAMES

SAYS

"I Can Help"

by Crystal Bowman
illustrated by Karen Maizel

ZondervanPublishingHouse
Grand Rapids, Michigan

A Division of HarperCollinsPublishers

Requests for information should be addressed to:
Zondervan Publishing House
Grand Rapids, Michigan 49530

Library of Congress Cataloging-in-Publication Data

Bowman, Crystal.
    Jonathan James says, "I can help" / by Crystal Bowman.
      p. cm. — (Jonathan James)
    Summary: Jonathan the rabbit learns that being a helper includes more
than just working with his mom and dad to clean house.
    ISBN: 0-310-49611-X
    [1. Rabbits—Fiction.   2. Helpfulness—Fiction.   3. Family life—Fiction.
4. Christian Life—Fiction.]   I. Title.   II. Series: Bowman, Crystal.
Jonathan James.
PZ7.B6834Jop 1995
[E]—dc20   95-6662
                                             CIP
                                           AC

Edited by Lori J. Walburg and Leslie Kimmelman
Cover design by Steven M. Scott
Art direction by Chris Gannon
Illustrations and interior design by Karen Maizel

95 96 97 98 99 /❖ DP / 10 9 8 7 6 5 4 3 2

For Grandma Langejans,
Grandma Bowman,
Dorene Hammes,
and Aunt Norm

—C. B.

For Annalie,
Cailen, and Cara,
my pride...
and who also helped
—K. M.

CONTENTS

NOT YET

"It is a nice sunny day today,"
said Jonathan James.

"Yes," said Mother.

"It is a very nice day."

"It would be a good day
to go to the park," said Jonathan.

"Yes, it would," Mother replied.

"But the house is a mess.
I must clean it today."

"Well," said Jonathan,

"may we go to the park
after you clean the house?"

"That would be fine," said Mother.

So Jonathan waited
while Mother cleaned the kitchen.

"May we go to the park now?"
asked Jonathan.

"Not yet," Mother answered.

"You'd better find something to do."

Jonathan got out his coloring book.

He colored two pictures.

"May we go to the park now?"
asked Jonathan.

"Not yet," said Mother.

"I need to clean the living room."

Jonathan looked at a book.

"May we go to the park now?"
he asked.

"Not yet," answered Mother.

"I need to clean the bathroom."

Jonathan played with his little
sister, Kelly.

"May we go to the park now?"
he asked.
"Not yet," said Mother.
"I need to clean the bedrooms."
Jonathan had an idea.
He would be a helper.
Being a helper would make
Mother happy.
It would make Jesus happy too.

Jonathan went into his bedroom.

It was a mess!

First he picked up his toys.

Next he made his bed.

Then he hung up his clothes.

He even dusted his dresser.

Mother was cleaning Kelly's bedroom.
"May we go to the park now?"
asked Jonathan.
"Not yet," said Mother.
"May we go after you clean my room?"
asked Jonathan.
"Yes," answered Mother.
"After I clean your room,
we will go to the park."

Mother went to Jonathan's bedroom.

"Surprise!" said Jonathan.

"Oh, my!" Mother exclaimed.

"Your room is so clean!

It looks very nice, J.J.

Thank you for being a helper."

"You're welcome," said Jonathan.

"Now may we go to the park?"

"Not yet," said Mother.

"But you said we could!"

cried Jonathan.

"After I get my sunglasses,

we will go to the park," said Mother.

Jonathan laughed.

"I will get mine too," he said.

So they put on their sunglasses

and went to the park.

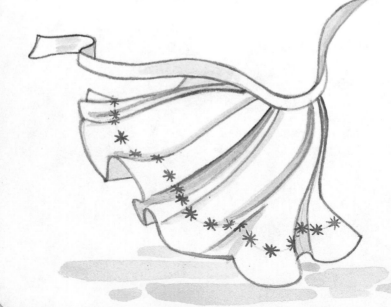

THE SLIVER

"Where is Father?" asked Jonathan.

"In his workroom," answered Mother.

"He is fixing a chair."

"I will help him," Jonathan said.

"Good idea," said Mother.

Jonathan went to Father's workroom.

"Need any help?" he asked.

"Oh, yes!" Father replied.

"You may hold the chair

while I fix the leg."

Jonathan liked helping Father.

He liked being in Father's workroom.

He liked looking at all of the tools.

"May I use your saw?"

asked Jonathan.

"Yes, you may," Father answered,

"but I will help you."

Father helped Jonathan use the saw.

It was fun.

"That is enough for now," said Father.

"You may use the saw again,

but only when I am here to help."

"All right," Jonathan agreed.

Jonathan went outdoors to play.

He went to Jason's house.

"Hello, Jason," said Jonathan.

"Hello," said Jason.

"Do you want play?" asked Jonathan.

"There is nothing to do," said Jason.

"Well," said Jonathan,

"we could go to my house."

"What can we do at your house?"
asked Jason.

"I could show you our tools,"
said Jonathan.

"Okay," Jason agreed.

"Let's go to your house."

So Jonathan and Jason
went to Jonathan's house.
They went into Father's workroom.
"Father lets me use his saw,"
said Jonathan.
"Let me try!" said Jason.
"Oh, no," said Jonathan.
"Father is not here to help us."

Jason took the saw anyway.

"Here," he said, "you hold the board."

Jonathan held the board
while Jason used the saw.

"Ouch!" cried Jonathan.

"I have a sliver in my finger.
Put the saw down."

"Fine," said Jason.

"I have to go home now anyway."

That night Father asked,

"J.J., did you use the saw?"

"No," Jonathan lied.

"Hmmm," said Father,

"someone moved it."

Jonathan felt awful!

He knew that he was lying.

"Why do you have a bandage
on your finger?" asked Father.
"I have a sliver," said Jonathan.
"Well," said Father,
"slivers need to come out,
or they will keep on hurting."

Father got a needle
from the sewing basket.
"There," he said, "the sliver is out.
Now your finger will feel better."
Jonathan started to cry.
"I got the sliver
in your workroom," he said.
"Jason and I were using the saw."
"Oh?" asked Father.
"Yes," said Jonathan.
"I'm sorry I lied.
I feel awful inside!"

"Well," said Father,
"lies are like slivers.
They will keep on hurting you
until you get rid of them.
I'm glad you told me the truth, J.J.,
but you must tell God
you are sorry too."
"Then will I feel better inside?"
asked Jonathan.
"Yes, you will," said Father.
Jonathan prayed.
He told God he was sorry
for telling a lie.
When Jonathan finished praying,
he opened his eyes.

"There!" said Jonathan.
"Now that lie can't
hurt me anymore."
Father smiled
and gave Jonathan a big hug.

THE INDOOR PICNIC

Jonathan woke up early.
Today his family was going
to the beach.
Jonathan put on his clothes
and packed his beach bag.
He went to the kitchen.
"When are we leaving?"
asked Jonathan.
"Where are we going?" asked Father.
"Today we are going to the beach,"
said Jonathan.
"Don't you remember?"

"Look out the window,"
said Mother.

Jonathan looked out the window.

"Oh, no!" cried Jonathan.

"It is raining.

Our day is ruined!"

"Our day is not ruined,"
said Mother.
"We will still have fun.
We will go to the beach tomorrow."
Jonathan was mad.
"Who needs rain anyway!" he said.
"We do," Mother answered.
"God sends the rain
to water the ground.
It helps the food to grow."

"Yes," said Father.

"If it didn't rain

we wouldn't have

corn on the cob or strawberries."

Jonathan liked corn on the cob.

And he liked juicy, red strawberries.

"Well," said Jonathan,

"I guess rain is good sometimes.

But what are we going to do today?"

"We are going to clean
the basement," said Father.
"Cleaning the basement is work,"
Jonathan complained.
"It will be fun if we do it together,"
said Mother.
Jonathan didn't say anything.
What a bad day! he thought.
After breakfast they all went
down to the basement.
Mother told Jonathan and Kelly
to pick up their toys.
"Please put them
in the toy basket," she said.

Jonathan picked up his toys.

"Look!" he said.

"Here is my baseball.

And there is my fire truck.

I didn't know where they were."

Kelly found her yellow bear.

"Hi, bear," she said.

"Where have you been hiding?"

31

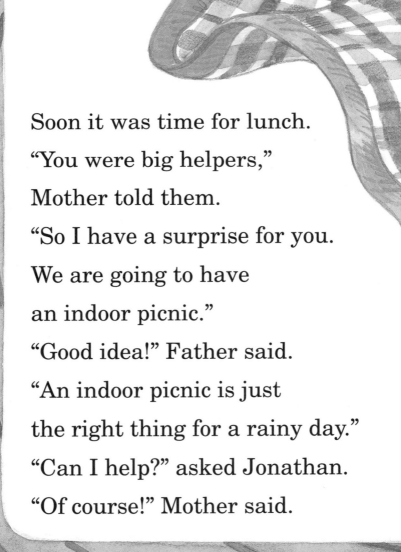

Soon it was time for lunch.

"You were big helpers,"
Mother told them.

"So I have a surprise for you.

We are going to have
an indoor picnic."

"Good idea!" Father said.

"An indoor picnic is just
the right thing for a rainy day."

"Can I help?" asked Jonathan.

"Of course!" Mother said.

Jonathan put a big blanket
on the floor.
Mother opened the picnic basket.
Then Jonathan and Kelly
passed out the plates and napkins.

"What are we having to eat?"
asked Jonathan.

"Well," said Mother,
"we have peanut butter sandwiches.
And thanks to the rain God sends,
we have corn on the cob."

"And for dessert," Father added,
"we have fresh strawberries
and cream."

"Oh, boy!" said Jonathan.

Jonathan was hungry.

He ate a peanut butter sandwich
and two ears of corn.

Then he had a big bowl
of strawberries and cream.

Jonathan liked having
an indoor picnic.
It was almost as much fun
as going to the beach.

JONATHAN TRIES TO HELP

Jonathan came to the breakfast table.
"Are we going to the beach today?"
asked Jonathan.

"Yes," Mother answered.
"It is a good day for the beach."

"When are we leaving?"
Jonathan asked.

"As soon as we are ready to go,"
Father replied.

"I will help," said Jonathan.

Jonathan helped Kelly

with her cereal.

But he spilled milk

all over the table.

What a mess!

"I will clean it up," Father said.

"I'm sorry," said Jonathan.

"I just wanted to help."

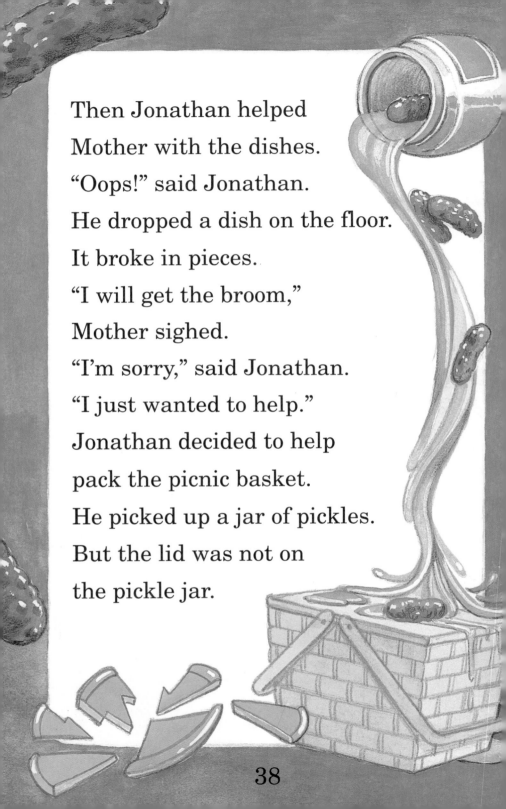

Then Jonathan helped
Mother with the dishes.
"Oops!" said Jonathan.
He dropped a dish on the floor.
It broke in pieces.
"I will get the broom,"
Mother sighed.
"I'm sorry," said Jonathan.
"I just wanted to help."
Jonathan decided to help
pack the picnic basket.
He picked up a jar of pickles.
But the lid was not on
the pickle jar.

Pickles spilled all over the basket.

"I will clean it up," Jonathan said.

"No," Mother said, "I do not
need your help right now."

Jonathan felt sad.

He went to his room
and shut the door.

Nobody wanted his help.

Knock, knock.

"Who's there?" he asked.

"Me," said Kelly.

"Do you want to play?"

"I want to help," said Jonathan.

"But I just get in the way."

Kelly took a book

from Jonathan's shelf.

"Will you read to me?" she asked.

"Okay," Jonathan agreed.

"There is nothing to do anyway."

Jonathan read the book to Kelly.

They read another book,

and then they read another one.

Knock, knock.

"Who is it?" Jonathan asked.

"It's me," Mother said.

"We are ready to go to the beach."

"Hooray!" cried Jonathan and Kelly.

When they got to the beach,
they found a good spot near the water.
Jonathan and Kelly
played in the sand.
"I will show you how
to make a sand castle,"
Jonathan told Kelly.

Then they splashed in the water.

"I will show you how to swim,"

said Jonathan.

Kelly and Jonathan had fun

swimming in the water.

Then they sat on their towels

in the warm sun.

Finally, it was time to go home.

"You were a big helper today,"
Father told Jonathan.

"No, I wasn't," Jonathan answered.

"I spilled milk on the table.
I broke a dish.
And I spilled pickles
all over the picnic basket."

"Those were just little accidents,"
Mother explained.

"That's right," said Father.
"You were a big helper
when you read to Kelly."

"Yes," Mother agreed.
"You helped Kelly
make a sand castle.
And you showed her how to swim."

"Well," Jonathan said,
"I guess I was a helper after all."
And he smiled happily.

Read Up on the Adventures of Jonathan James!

Jonathan James Says, "I Can Be Brave"

Book 1   ISBN 0-310-49591-1

Jonathan James is afraid. His new bedroom is too dark. He's going into first grade. And he has to stay at Grandma's overnight for the first time. What should he do? These four lively, humorous stories will show new readers that sometimes things that seemed scary can actually be fun.

Jonathan James Says, "Let's Be Friends"

Book 2   ISBN 0-310-49601-2

Jonathan James is making new friends! In four easy-to-read stories, Jonathan meets a missionary, a physically challenged boy, and a new neighbor. New readers will learn important lessons about friendship. And they will learn that our friends like us just for being who we are.

Jonathan James Says, "I Can Help"

Book 3   ISBN 0-310-49611-X

Jonathan James is growing up—and that means he can help! In four chapters written especially for new readers, Jonathan James learns to pitch in and help his family—sometimes successfully, sometimes not. Young readers will learn that they, too, have ways they can help.

Jonathan James Says, "Let's Play Ball"

Book 4   ISBN 0-310-49621-7

Jonathan James wants to learn how to play baseball. Who will teach him? Will he ever hit the ball? Four fun-filled chapters show young readers that, with practice, they too can succeed in whatever they try.

Look for all the books in the Jonathan James series at your local Christian bookstore.

ZondervanPublishingHouse

5300 Patterson S.E. • Grand Rapids, MI 49530

Crystal Bowman was born and raised in Holland, Michigan, where she lived in a neighborhood with lots of kids. Her favorite activities were jumping rope, playing hopscotch, and riding bikes with her friends. She now lives in Grand Rapids, Michigan, with her husband and children. She is the author of *Cracks in the Sidewalk*, a book of humorous poems for children.

Karen Maizel lives near Lake Erie in Ohio with her husband and three daughters. She has always had a love for drawing and colors. "My daughters are my best critics," Karen says. "They love to see my pictures before the readers do. Sometimes they even pose for me!" Karen's husband, Stan, also helps her come up with ideas. "I couldn't do my art without my family's help!" she says.

Crystal and Karen would love to hear from you. You may write them at:

Author Relations
Zondervan Publishing House
5300 Patterson Ave., S.E.
Grand Rapids, MI 49530